Won't You Come and Play with Me?

Adapted by Mary Lee Donovan • *Illustrated by* Cynthia Jabar

Houghton Mifflin Company
Boston 1998

Acknowledgments

I am extremely grateful to Jane Hart for publishing the original two verses in *Singing Bee* (Morrow, 1982) and for leading me to the source of the song, William Greene. And I am very grateful to Mr. Greene himself, who remembered the song so clearly from his post–World War I childhood in his Chicago neighborhood. And I must thank Anne Quirk, Morse Hamilton, Ann Rider, and my husband, Jed, whose enthusiasm helped turn this simple street rhyme into a story.

—M.L.D.

Text copyright © 1998 by Mary Lee Donovan
Illustrations copyright © 1998 by Cynthia Jabar

The text of this book is set in New Century Schoolbook.
The illustrations are scratchboard and watercolor on paper.

Library of Congress Cataloging-in-Publication Data

Donovan, Mary Lee.
    Won't you come and play with me? / adapted by Mary Lee Donovan; illustrated by Cynthia Jabar.
        p.   cm.
    Summary: A song that takes the speaker up to the barber shop, down through the village green, into the baker's shop, and eventually into Mother's arms.
    ISBN 0-395-84630-7
    1. Children's songs—Texts. [1. Songs.] I. Jabar, Cynthia, ill. II. Title.
PZ8.3.D726Wo 1998
782.42164'0268
[E]—dc21
                                                              97-2529
                                                              CIP
                                                              AC

Manufactured in the United States of America
WOZ 10 9 8 7 6 5 4 3 2 1

For my own sweet, spirited Nathaniel
— M.L.D.

For my mother — thanks for showing me how to be brave.
— C.J.

Up to the barber shop I go;
I cannot stay any longer,
for if I do, my mother will say
I played with the boys on the corner.

E-I-O for Willie,
E-I-O for Willie;
won't you come, won't you come,
won't you come and play with me?

Down through the village green I go —
a shortcut through the flowers;
for if I poke, my mother will say
I romped with the dogs for hours.

E-I-O for Flossie,
E-I-O for Flossie;
won't you come, won't you come,
won't you come and run with me?

Into the baker's shop I go;
I have to leave there quickly,
for if I'm slow, my mother will say
my face and hands got sticky.

E-I-O for Ivan,
E-I-O for Ivan;
won't you come, won't you come,
won't you come and bake for me?

Down to the corner store I go;
I cannot stop or dally,
for if I do, my mother will say
I gawked at the new girl, Sally.

E-I-O for Sally,
E-I-O for Sally;
won't you come, won't you come,
won't you come and marry me?

Down to the breezy bay I go
to catch some fish for supper,
but if I stay my mother will say
I sailed the restless harbor.

E-I-O for Johnny,
E-I-O for Johnny;
won't you come, won't you come,
won't you come and race with me?

Away to the dusty road I go,
the day is quickly fading.
Now I'm late and my mother will say
my bread and soup are waiting.

E-I-O for Mama,
E-I-O for Mama;
won't you come, won't you come,
won't you come and wait for me?

Into my mother's arms I go,
a wayward boy home safely.
But now I'm here and here I'll stay
for supper and a story.

E-I-O for Mama,
E-I-O for Mama;

won't you come, won't you come,
won't you come and sit by me?

E-I-O for Mama,
E-I-O for Mama;
won't you come, won't you come,
won't you come and stay with me?

Author's Note

Spontaneous street songs, rhymes, and games have long been a part of every childhood. Not very long ago, I feared that the ones I loved, invented, and changed endlessly with my neighborhood friends may have been the last gasps of the oral tradition. But I now know that children will continue the thread of playground lore that belongs so uniquely and personally to them for as long as they find time and space to play.

Though Nathan's roundabout trip to the barbershop is a fairly contemporary scenario, this call-to-play has its origins in other calls that go back much further than 1917 Chicago. As I developed the original two verses into a story, I tried to remain within the realm of possibility for a child of that time. However, I hope that children chanting this verse today will personalize it with the names of their own friends and the particulars of their own adventures, truant and otherwise!